A Battle of Brutes

A Lesson Learned

Nicolas J. Rillema
and
Josh Langston

Dedication

This book is dedicated to grandparents and grandkids everywhere. Let this be proof that just because there are quite a few years difference between their ages, the two can still work together and achieve something of which they can be justly proud.

Speaking as the senior member of a two-guy team, I could not be more happy or enthusiastic over the fact that my grandson Nick urged me to work with him. For an added detail or two, please check out Final Thoughts at the end.

Collaborations like ours need to be emulated!

Part One—Grumble's Aggression

Welcome to a battle between two of the biggest primates on Earth! A silverback gorilla named Grumbles and a Bornean orangutan known as Chomp (for the peculiar noise he makes when angered). Though these two are not natural enemies—their habitats are thousands of miles apart—they are here now to see who can beat who, and perhaps, how.

They take up their positions; Grumbles hulks down on a flat-topped boulder, while Chomp sits on the lowest branch of an ancient tree.

First, meet Grumbles, the silverback gorilla, as he postures angrily at the orangutan. Someone in the crowd of excited watchers calls out, "Go get him, G-back!"

The gorilla stands upright and pounds his chest, creating a staccato of thumps, a scary rhythm of mayhem. He believes himself the most dominant creature in the forest. (Others, male lions among them, might disagree.)

Chomp merely yawns; he's utterly dismissive of the silver-gray beast in front of him. The orangutan stretches his extremely long, hairy arms to the max. Having survived to adulthood without being eaten by leopards, crocodiles, or pythons, this Bornean behemoth isn't worried about the upcoming battle. If anything, he looks bored.

Grumbles takes notice of the orangutan's lackadaisical attitude, and it only angers him more. He's ready, whether or not his shaggy, red opponent is.

Both of these competitors have a common diet, meaning they mostly eat insects and plants. The orangutan considers ants to be a delicacy. This particular gorilla favors ripe bananas with his bugs.

In size, Grumbles has a distinct advantage. Considered an adult at the age of 12, his weight-to-strength ratio is among the highest of any living animal. A mountain gorilla has one especially significant advantage: he can bite with a force of 1,300 pounds per square inch. He stands five feet tall and weighs 430 pounds, virtually all of it muscle. When he roars, everyone listens!

Except perhaps, the orangutan. He's busy eating a stick covered in ants and isn't particularly interested in the gorilla's physical prowess.

That might be a mistake since Chomp is a good bit smaller. Though about the same height as Grumbles, the 200-pound orangutan is less than half his weight. His arm span, however, is slightly over seven feet. While not as strong as the gorilla, he is much more agile when it comes to traveling through the forest, swinging from branch to branch with both speed and agility. His strength is easily seven times that of a male human.

Grumbles is supremely confident; he knows he's going to win. No other outcome, in his mind, is possible.

Chomp is counting on this and has planned ahead. He has a surprise or two in store for the over-confident silverback.

At the start of the match, Grumbles hurries toward the orangutan's tree, looks up at him, and pounds on his chest to declare victory in a match that has yet to begin.

The orangutan looks down and spits on him which only enrages Grumbles more. The silverback tries to reach the limb on which the orangutan sits, but he can't quite reach it, even when he jumps. That further annoys the gorilla but pleases the orangutan who simply reaches down from his perch and punches the gorilla's head every time he leaps.

After several successful punches, Grumbles changes tactics. He looks around for something with which to knock down the orangutan's tree. He settles on a boulder (gorillas can lift as much as 4,000 pounds) and hauls it toward the tree. Grunting with effort, he lifts the huge stone to his chest and heaves it at the tree.

<Whump!>

The tree shudders, and Chomp has to use both arms to keep from falling.

<Whump!>

The tree begins to lean back toward the jungle.

<Whump! Whump!>

The gorilla keeps up his attack until the tree is leaning at a steep angle. As he picks up the boulder for one final, tree-downing throw, the orangutan leaps toward an alternate hardwood while making orangutan giggle sounds.

Grumbles goes nearly insane with anger because the orangutan simply refuses to cooperate and present himself for execution!

His anger rising to levels he never before experienced, Grumbles races toward the new tree only to be clobbered again, but this time the orangutan uses a heavy branch, and he swings it like a sledgehammer.

<Thump! Thump!>

Now the gorilla is both angry and frustrated. He grabs the boulder he used before and moves as quickly as he can toward his enemy.

As soon as Grumbles gets close enough to the tree, Chomp whacks him again. The gorilla staggers backward, holding his throbbing noggin.

Chomp thinks this is hysterically funny and jumps down from the tree with the heavy branch still clutched in his hairy fist.

Though Grumbles is still reeling from the never-before-experienced head bashing, he sees his chance at last—the

orangutan is finally down on the gorilla's turf. Grumbles' lip curls into a sneer.

Chomp quickly realizes his terrible mistake and pees right on the spot.

The gorilla advances quickly, still thumping his chest, but slips on the puddle of urine in his path. As soon as he goes down, the orangutan leaps back up into the woods and swings gracefully through the treetops hoping to enrage the gorilla even more.

Unfortunately for Chomp, the tree he's chosen isn't very thick. Grumbles stretches to his full height, bears down on the trunk of the tree, and violently shakes it. Suddenly, the orangutan is dislodged. He tries to leap to another tree, but he can't make it all the way. He's off balance and plummets toward the ground.

Grumbles wasn't prepared for an orangutan to land on top of him and was stunned by the 200-pound turn of events. But he isn't the only one to suffer from the fall; Chomp is groggy, too.

It becomes a race to see which of the two fighters can recover quickly enough to take advantage of the other's injuries.

Grumbles' eyes open; he shakes his head and looks at the downed orangutan. His opponent then wakes up, too, and faces an enraged gorilla with hatred in his eyes and heart.

A pair of African grey parrots land nearby to observe the battle. The orangutan is tossed around by the gorilla. Chomp manages to get in a punch or two, but the conflict is fully in Grumbles' control.

The birds chatter a bit, and Grumbles growls at them.

Fortunately for Chomp, the parrots figured things out before the orangutan did; at that point, he wasn't thinking clearly at all. But he knew he could not win and struggled to get away.

The birds point Chomp in the right direction–the deep jungle, and the high trees. Finally, he could rest and recover.

Part Two–Chomp's Revenge

The jungle can be a dark and scary place, especially if it's not *your* jungle. That was just one of the problems faced by Chomp, a bold Bornean orangutan who traveled over 5,000 miles to face a challenge with a silverback gorilla named Grumbles. Their first battle had raged back and forth, which stunned not only the spectators but to 430-pound Grumbles as well.

It took a while for Chomp to recover. He felt sure Grumbles needed time, too, since Chomp had landed enough blows to destroy one of his fellow tree dwellers.

None of that was on Chomp's mind at the time. It embarrassed him that everyone saw him run away at the end of the fight. He had traveled alone and had few friends. The only exception was the pair of African grey parrots that helped him escape.

9

But they had also expected more from Chomp, even though gorillas are bigger and stronger than orangutans. The parrots shared Chomp's belief that orangutans, while smaller, were also smarter. In fact, the birds indicated to Chomp that they were disappointed in him.

That haunted him all during his brief recovery. So did memories of Grumbles pounding on his chest, huffing and grunting one threat after another. Chomp knew he had to even the score.

That's why he made it known to the promoter who arranged the fight, Myron Froghammer, that he wanted another chance at Grumbles. The spectators who watched the first battle were eager to see another go-round, too.

When Grumbles heard about it, he cackled like a howler monkey, though no one dared tell him that. He proclaimed himself the victor. He did not need or want to face the orangutan again.

The promoter howled back at him using his secret method of communication, "Are you afraid? Are you a chicken? You didn't finish the orangutan last time. What makes you think you can beat him this time?"

Such remarks touched a nerve—several nerves to be exact. Grumbles flew into a rage, as he always did when he didn't get his way. He then demanded a re-match, too. The sooner the better.

The event was scheduled quickly, and word went out to everyone who came to the first match. It seemed like no one knew how to tell the nosey parrots. Fortunately, Chomp did.

He had one week to get ready. And while he thought he'd planned ahead the first time; he swore to do better in round two. The one thing he counted on, besides his own cleverness, was Grumble's thick-headed swagger, and his inability to control his temper. By the time the match started, Chomp was quite ready.

Just as he had before, Chomp sat in a tree looking down on Grumbles who was stomping around and acting like he'd already won. Chomp shook his head as if to say, "Oh, you poor, poor gorilla. You are in for a big surprise."

Without waiting for Grumbles to engage him, Chomp used a stout vine and took a running leap which sent him on

a dazzling arc through the air. He let go and landed just behind a spot he'd located earlier and begged the gorilla to come after him.

Grumbles did so, hustling forward on all fours with his head up and his chest low to the ground.

Chomp grabbed a stick he'd placed nearby and stirred up a hornet's nest that Grumbles was about to step on. The insects were infuriated when the gorilla arrived, and they let him have it.

Suddenly, Grumbles had a swarm of angry insects stinging him all over. Meanwhile, Chomp moved away from the ambush but stayed close enough to hear the gorilla groan, roar, and swat at the swarm. He beat his chest, too, but for a very different reason.

Finally, the gorilla sprawled into a nearby stream and slathered himself with mud. Once done, he sat in the brown water with only his head and shoulders exposed. The hornets soon left. The gorilla made it quite clear that he was annoyed, terribly, terribly annoyed.

Chomp ate a banana from a bunch he had stashed nearby. The full stalk held many clumps of bright yellow fruit, the gorilla's favorite. Chomp's sighs of pleasure angered Grumbles who stalked out of the stream and shook off water and mud.

He immediately focused on the orangutan gorging himself on one big banana after another. He had one in each hand and several more in his lap. *That was Grumbles' food! Stolen from one of his trees!*

The great ape narrowed his eyes, growled, and began another attack.

Chomp faked being afraid. He looked around, as if hoping to find a hiding place, then suddenly ran, angling toward an opening in the jungle.

Grumbles chased him. The thief was foolishly trying to escape on the ground! He might have had a chance among the treetops, but he stayed on the jungle floor—what a stupid, stupid mistake!

Chomp carried some bananas which he dropped one-by-one as he ran. He doubted the gorilla would stop for one or two such treats, that's why he'd previously put a dozen of them on a spot of ground covered by palm fronds. As soon as he'd leaped over them, the wily orangutan climbed up into the safety of the trees.

Grumbles slowed down when he saw his opponent climb a tree. He'd given the rascal a huge scare, and his reward was piled right in front of him—an entire meal of bananas—just waiting for him. He decided to let the stupid orangutan waste away in the woods while he enjoyed a massive snack.

Exactly three steps later, and before Grumbles could even pick up his prize, the ground collapsed under him. Along with the bananas and the palm leaves, he fell into a hole the "stupid" orangutan had enlarged and hidden. The five-foot-tall gorilla tried to grab the edge and crawl out, but he couldn't reach it, even when he jumped.

He was NOT happy.

But Chomp was jubilant! He rocked back and forth on his perch until the two friendly African grey parrots landed next to him. Through squawks and gestures, they warned him about a stout but loose vine nearby.

The orangutan, however, was too busy congratulating himself and ignored them. Minutes later, he accidentally knocked the vine loose, and the end of it swept over and down into the gorilla hole.

Chomp grabbed his end of the vine to yank it out, but he was too late. Grumbles grasped it firmly between his two massive fists, and in no time had crawled out.

Suddenly a massive bolt of lightning lit the sky. The thunder that followed made the spectators scramble for cover.

Myron Froghammer, the promoter waved his arms and shouted, "The battle is postponed until tomorrow!"

Part Three—It Ain't Over 'til it's Over

Communication is the hardest part of organizing battles between members of similar species. Myron Froghammer, a rich promoter of such fights, often complained about it, but he managed to do it somehow and then refused to share his secrets. Though no one else knew it, his methods were neither quick nor foolproof.

This became obvious when his latest combatants, a silverback gorilla and a Bornean orangutan totally ignored his notice that their match had been postponed. If given a bit more time, he might have checked with the fighters before he said anything. Neither Chomp, the orangutan, nor Grumbles, the gorilla, wanted to stop.

As the thunderstorm that delayed round two came to an end, Chomp raced up a coconut tree and bombarded Grumbles with coconuts while the gorilla looked up at him and made threats. He soon realized that Chomp was a master at hurling hard, brown nuts at the gorilla's head. Few missed their mark even though Grumbles moved around the tree trunk to avoid the cannonball-sized missiles.

He used all his great strength to shake the tree and dislodge the orangutan. But the tree hardly budged, and the bombing went on until the last coconut was gone. Chomp scratched his head briefly, then leaped to another coconut tree nearby and continued the barrage.

Grumbles tried to throw the huge nuts back at Chomp, but his aim was terrible. Barely one in ten even reached the orangutan who simply caught them and sent them hurtling back down. The gorilla had no choice but to quit.

Covering his head as he ran, Grumbles hurried past all the pitfalls and traps he'd faced before and almost made it to Froghammer's trailer when the hornets once again caught him. He reached the trailer and pounded on the door while swatting at the stinging insects all around him.

Unwilling to admit defeat, he growled at Froghammer and held up three fingers to indicate he wanted another chance, a tie-breaker.

"That's excellent—I can sell even more tickets!" Exclaimed the fat, greedy promoter. Using his secret method of communication, he told Grumbles the event would take place the next day. Grumbles then headed back to the safety of the now even muddier stream where he attempted to drown the hornets.

Fortunately for Chomp, the African Grey parrots saw the whole thing, flew up into the coconut tree, and alerted him. Once again, Chomp vowed to be ready.

The crowd of spectators arrived early the next morning, eager to watch what Froghammer promised would be a fight to the death.

Right on time, Grumbles appeared and made all his usual noises and threats.

Chomp came from the opposite direction, with a tree limb heavily covered in ripe bananas on his shoulder. Upon seeing the bananas, Grumbles stretched both of his massive arms in front of his chest, palms out, and shook his head from side to side. He wanted nothing more to do with bananas.

His rejection of the fruit lasted just long enough for Chomp to start throwing them at him. Grumbles took the first one in his face, then answered the challenge by throwing it back at the orangutan. That set off a battle of bananas, most of which were picked up and re-thrown. Neither of them felt much pain since the bright yellow fruit had already turned slightly soft.

The crowd, however, turned slightly angry. No. Actually, they got *seriously* angry. They wanted to see mayhem, madness, and murder, all the grim things Froghammer had promised. There were cries of "Where is that jerk?" and "Why can't fat old Froggy come out and *do* something?"

Someone near the edge of the crowd shouted, "Look! He's getting away!" A cloud of oily, black smoke blossomed from behind the promoter's truck as he cranked the engine.

Outraged, the crowd surged toward the vehicle, leaving the gorilla and the orangutan staring at each other amid a field littered with bananas. They each took a seat and started eating them.

Meanwhile, the angry spectators surrounded Froghammer's truck. They grew even more angry when they saw all the cash the fat promoter had stacked on the seat beside him. The crowd pounded on the truck. Someone smashed the headlights with a rock. Others grabbed rocks of their own and smashed all the windows.

Froghammer used his arms to protect his face from flying glass, whimpering all the while. Soon, the crowd yanked his door open and dragged him out. His whimpers turned to screams as if he'd been set on fire.

When his protests didn't work, he thrashed about, punching and biting anyone who touched him. At last, he broke free. He pushed people out of his way, running and stumbling over them as he headed for safety in the jungle.

As the battle between the humans grew more heated, Grumbles and Chomp became the spectators. The bananas tasted even better when they could eat them while watching the show.

Froghammer's lumbering jog brought him close to the two apes. Chomp

reached out one long arm and grabbed the fleeing fat man by the ankle. He went down as if hit by a rhino. Chomp dragged him toward Grumbles who reached for Froghammer's chubby arms. Between them, they lifted the screaming schemer off the ground and tossed him back toward the crowd.

The spectators roared their approval. Chomp and Grumbles were shocked by the turn of events, but they realized it represented a wonderful opportunity for them to get their revenge on the promoter. They ambled toward him, their eyes gleaming.

"Wait! Stop!" cried Froghammer. "Can't we settle this with cash? I have money, lots and lots of—"

He stopped talking when his two hairy opponents picked him up once again.

The crowd began to chant, "Toss him; toss him; toss him around!" They wanted the promoter punished. And while the two huge animals couldn't understand their words, they certainly understood their desire.

After throwing Froghammer away from the crowd, Chomp and Grumbles took turns tossing him back and forth, all to the cheers of the human mob watching them.

Distant sirens caused them to slow down. Moments later, the police arrived with an ambulance, and the officers ended the beating.

The crowd stepped in when the police tried to punish the two fighters. But once they understood what Froghammer had done, they agreed to let Chomp and Grumbles go.

The promoter had no say in the matter since he had been knocked out cold. The local police and the ambulance left together while the spectators argued over the money left in Froghammer's truck.

Grumbles and Chomp traded puzzled looks; neither cared to go on fighting. The two parrots floated in and separated when they reached the former combatants. One landed on Chomp's shoulder, and the other landed on Grumbles.

After gathering double handfuls of the less damaged bananas, the former enemies walked into the jungle together. They needed to find a place in the shade where they could relax and share their feast with the parrots.

~The End~

A Battle of Brutes

Nicholas J. Rillema and Josh Langston

F inal Thoughts

At the ripe old age of ten, my grandson Nicolas Rillema, asked me if we could write a story together. He had an idea in mind, and knowing that I've written quite a few novels, he thought a collaboration was in order.

I was immediately charmed by the idea but cautioned that if we were going to write a story, it had to be worth reading. It had to be interesting, imaginative, and most importantly, fun!

We worked together on the plot during a vacation stay in Washington state, then continued our collaboration online, sharing thoughts and discussing all sorts of sneaky tricks we could pull on our characters. I should never have worried that Nick might run out of ideas. He didn't! Nor did I ever imagine how much fun such a collaboration could be.

At the time, Nick was 10, and I was 73. But for some reason, that didn't bother either of us. We weren't about to let a mere six decade age difference slow us down. We put a lot into the job, and we're both very pleased with it.

Nick allowed me to go over the final draft and spruce it up for publication. I posted the original on my blog, but this version benefits from additional stock images and some others generated by the impressive AI graphics engine I found at 123rf.com.

The snapshot below is of my storytelling partner working his way through the woods during our trip to the Olympic National Forest. I can't imagine where he gets all his crazy ideas, but I'm sure glad he gets 'em!

Well done, Nick. Well done.

A Battle of Brutes